WATCHMAN NEE

NEW BELIEVER'S SERIES

MEETING

10

Living Stream Ministry
Anaheim, California

© 1993 Living Stream Ministry

All rights reserved. No part of this work may be reproduced or transmitted in any form or by any means—graphic, electronic, or mechanical, including photocopying, recording, or information storage and retrieval systems—without written permission from the publisher.

First Edition, November 1997.

ISBN 1-57593-966-5

Published by

Living Stream Ministry
2431 W. La Palma Ave., Anaheim, CA 92801 U.S.A.
P. O. Box 2121, Anaheim, CA 92814 U.S.A.

Printed in the United States of America

02 03 04 05 / 10 9 8 7 6 5 4 3

MEETING

Scripture Reading: Heb. 10:25; Matt. 18:20; Acts 2:42; 1 Cor. 14:23, 26

I. CORPORATE GRACE BEING FOUND IN THE MEETING

God's Word says, "Not abandoning our own assembling together" (Heb. 10:25). Why should we not abandon the assembling together? Because God dispenses His grace to us through the assembling together. God's grace to man can be divided into two categories—personal and corporate. God gives us not only personal grace but also corporate grace. This corporate grace can be found only in the assembling together or the meetings.

We have already spoken of the subject of prayer. One can learn to pray by himself at home; there is no doubt that God listens to such prayers. God listens to individual prayers. However, there is another kind of prayer. In order for this other kind of prayer to be answered, it must be prayed in the meetings, in the principle of two or three asking together in the Lord's name. If a person tries to do this alone, he will not get any answer. Many great matters must be prayed over in the meetings before God will answer. They must be brought to the prayer meeting before we see them come to pass. God's corporate grace comes to man only through the meetings. You may think that it is sufficient for a man to pray alone and that he can seek God's mercy by himself. But the experience of many people tells us that individual prayers alone will not work. It seems that unless two or three people pray, or all the brothers and sisters come together to pray, God will not answer. Therefore, we have two kinds of answers to prayers: One is answer to individual prayers, and the other is answer to assembly prayers. If we do not meet with others, some prayers will not be answered.

We have also spoken of reading the Bible. Of course, God will give us individual grace when we read the Bible. However, some portions of the Word cannot be opened up by one person alone. God gives light when we meet, when we assemble ourselves together. In such a meeting, some brothers may be led to open up a particular portion of the Word. There may not be any speaking concerning that particular portion of the Word, yet the fact that everyone is assembled together gives God the opportunity to shed His light. Many brothers and sisters can testify that they understand more of God's Word in the meeting than when they study it individually. Many times in the meeting, God opens up one portion of the Word through another portion of the Word. As one person speaks on one passage, light shines on another passage. In this way more light is unveiled, and we receive grace in a corporate way.

If we do not meet with others, the most we can have is individual grace; we will miss a great part of the corporate grace. God will only give us corporate grace in the meeting. If we do not meet with others, we will not receive this grace. This is why the Bible charges us not to abandon our assembling together.

II. THE CHURCH AND THE MEETING

One outstanding characteristic of the church is that it meets. A Christian can never substitute meetings with "self-taught" pursuits. God has a category of grace reserved for the meetings only. If we do not meet with others, that portion of corporate grace will not be available to us.

In the Old Testament God commanded the Israelites to meet. In many places in the Bible they are called *the congregation*. That they were called a congregation meant they had to meet together. When we come to the New Testament, the revelation is even clearer. We have the clear commandment not to abandon "our own assembling together." God is not that interested in individuals being "self-taught." We must assemble ourselves together before we can receive His corporate grace. No forsaker of meetings will keep His grace. It is a foolish thing to abandon assembling together. A man must meet; he must come together with other children of God before he can receive the corporate grace.

The Bible gives explicit commandments as well as clear examples of people meeting together. When the Lord was on the earth, He often met with His disciples. He met with them on the mountain (Matt. 5:1), in the wilderness (Mark 6:32-34), at home (2:1-2), and at the seaside (4:1). On the last evening before His crucifixion, He borrowed a large upper room and met with the disciples (14:15-17). After His resurrection, He appeared in the midst of their gathering (John 20:19, 26; Acts 1:4). Before the day of Pentecost, the disciples gathered together in one accord to pray (v. 14). When the day of Pentecost came, they were also gathered together (2:1). After that they continued steadfastly in the teaching and fellowship of the apostles, in the breaking of bread and the prayers. Shortly thereafter, they were persecuted and went back to their own places. Yet they still met together (4:23-31). After Peter was released, he went to the house where the disciples were gathered together (12:12). First Corinthians 14 tells us clearly that the whole church gathered together (v. 23). It was *the whole church* that gathered together. No one who is part of the church can be exempt from meeting together with the church.

What is the meaning of the word *church*? The word *church* is *ekklesia* in Greek. *Ek* means "to come out," while *klesia* means "to congregate or to gather." Thus, *ekklesia* means the gathering of those who have been called out. God is not only after some called out ones; He wants the called out ones to gather together. If all the called out ones are separated from one another, we will not have the church; the church will not be produced.

After we have believed in the Lord there is a basic need we must take care of, that is, to come together with other children of God. We should never have the strange thought that we can be "self-taught" Christians. We must eliminate such a thought from our mind. Christianity does not have "self-taught" Christians; it only has the gathering of the whole church. Do not think that we can be Christians who just shut ourselves up to pray and to read the Bible alone at home. Christianity is not built on just individuals but also on the assembling together.

III. THE FUNCTIONING OF THE BODY MANIFESTED THROUGH THE MEETING

First Corinthians 12 speaks of the Body, and chapter fourteen speaks of the meeting. Chapter twelve speaks of the gifts of the Holy Spirit, and chapter fourteen also speaks of the gifts of the Holy Spirit. Chapter twelve speaks of the gifts in the Body, whereas chapter fourteen speaks of the gifts in the church. According to these two chapters, it seems that the mutual functioning of the members of the Body is expressed in the meeting. When we put chapters twelve and fourteen together, we see clearly that chapter twelve shows us the Body while chapter fourteen shows us the Body in function. One chapter speaks of the Body, while the other speaks of the meeting. One speaks of the gifts in the Body, while the other speaks of the gifts in the meeting. The functioning of the Body is realized specifically through the meeting. The mutual help, mutual influence, and mutual care of the members (e.g., the eyes helping the legs, the ears helping the hands, the hands helping the mouth) are more clearly manifested in the meetings. Through the meeting, we receive many answers to prayer. We often receive no light individually. But when we come to the meeting, we find light. What we see individually through our own pursuit can never match what we see in the meetings. All the ministries ordained by God operate through the meeting and are for the meeting. If a person rarely meets with others, he will have little opportunity to realize the functioning of the Body.

In addition to being the Body of Christ, the church is also the dwelling place of God. In the Old Testament the light of God was in the Holy of Holies. There was sunlight in the outer court, and there was the lamp with olive oil burning before the veil in the Holy Place. But in the Holy of Holies, there was no natural or artificial light. There was only the light of God. The Holy of Holies is the place where God dwells.

Wherever God dwells, there is His light. Today when the church gathers together as the dwelling place of God, we find God's light. When the church meets together, God manifests His light. We do not know why this happens. We can say only that this is one of the results of the mutual functioning of the members. The mutual functioning allows God's light to be expressed through the Body.

Deuteronomy 32:30 says, "How shall one chase a thousand, / And two put ten thousand to flight, / Were it not that their Rock sold them, / And Jehovah delivered them up?" If one could chase a thousand, how could two put ten thousand to flight? This is a strange thing. We do not know how, but we know that this is a fact. According to man, if one can chase a thousand, two should be able to chase only two thousand. But God says two can chase ten thousand, which is eight thousand more. When two chase separately, each can chase a thousand. Putting the two together, we should only have two thousand. But when two are joined together to chase the enemy, we have the mutual functioning of the members, and they can chase ten thousand, eight thousand more than if it is done separately. A person who does not know the Body and who does not care about meeting together will lose the eight thousand. Therefore, we need to learn to receive corporate grace. Do not think that personal grace is enough. We repeat: A special characteristic of Christianity is that it meets. A Christian can never substitute meeting with "self-taught" pursuits. We need to see this clearly and pay attention to it.

The Lord promises us two kinds of presence. One is in Matthew 28, and the other is in Matthew 18. In Matthew 28:20 the Lord said, "I am with you all the days until the consummation of the age." One can say that this implies His presence in individuals. In Matthew 18:20 the Lord said, "For where there are two or three gathered into My name, there am I in their midst." His presence here refers to His presence in the meeting. Only in the meeting can we have this second kind of presence. The Lord's presence with an individual and His presence in the meeting are two different things. Some only know the Lord's presence as individuals. But this knowledge is insufficient. The more compelling and powerful presence is experienced only in the meeting; we cannot experience such a presence individually. Although individually we can have the Lord's presence, this presence is never as great or as powerful as His presence in the meetings. But when we are among the saints we can touch a presence which we could not otherwise experience as individuals. We have to learn to meet together with the brothers and sisters because it is in the meeting that we experience the Lord's special presence. This is a tremendous blessing. This presence can never be felt by us as individuals. It is impossible to find a "self-taught" Christian who can experience this kind of powerful presence of the Lord.

It is a spontaneous thing for God's children to function in mutuality when they come together. We do not know how this mutuality in the Body works in the meeting, but we know that this mutuality is a fact. When one brother stands up, others see the light. When another brother stands up, others feel the Lord's presence. One brother opens his mouth to pray and others touch God. Another brother speaks a few words and others feel the supply of life. This phenomenon cannot be explained by human words; it surpasses human explanation. Only when the Lord comes back will we really know how the Body of Christ functions in mutuality. Today we merely obey the Lord's ordination.

Perhaps you have not paid much attention to the meeting because you have just been saved. You do not know what the light of the Body is and what the function and efficacy of the Body is. However, experience tells us that many fundamental spiritual lessons are learned only in the Body. The more you meet, the more you learn. If you do not meet, you have no part at all in these riches. Therefore, we hope that you will learn to meet properly from the very beginning of your Christian life.

IV. THE PRINCIPLES OF MEETING

How should we meet? The first principle in the Bible concerning meetings is that all meetings are conducted in the Lord's name. Matthew 18:20 says, "Gathered into My name," which can also be translated as, "Gathered under My name." What does it mean to be gathered under the Lord's name? It means to be under the Lord's authority. The Lord is the center, and everyone is drawn to Him. We do not go to a meeting to visit certain brothers or sisters, nor do we go because we are attracted by certain brothers or sisters. We go to the meeting to be gathered together with other saints under the Lord's name. The Lord is the center. We do not meet to listen to someone's preaching but to meet the Lord. If you meet to listen to someone's preaching, I am afraid you are coming under that person's name, not under the Lord's name. Sometimes, men's names are used to attract people. This is to draw men under that person's name. But the Lord says that we have to meet under His name.

We should come under the Lord's name because the Lord is not with us in a physical sense (Luke 24:5-6). Whenever the Lord is not physically present, there is the need of His name. When the Lord is physically present, there is less of a need for His name. The name is present because the person Himself is not present. As far as His physical body is concerned, the Lord is in heaven. Yet He has left us with a name. The Lord has promised that if we meet under His name, He will be in our midst. This means that His Spirit will be in our midst. Although the Lord is sitting in heaven, His name is still in our midst, and His Spirit is also in our midst. The Holy Spirit is the One who upholds the Lord's name. The Holy Spirit is the guardian of Christ's name; He protects and guards the Lord's name. Wherever there is the name of the Lord, there is the Holy Spirit, and there the Lord's name is manifested. Those who want to meet must meet under the Lord's name.

The second principle of meeting is that its goal should be for the building up of others. In 1 Corinthians 14 Paul told us that the basic principle of meeting is to build up others, not ourselves. Everything in the meeting should be for the purpose of building up others, not ourselves. Tongue speaking builds up the speaker, but the interpretation of tongues builds up others. In other words, every move that builds up just one person is in the principle of tongue-speaking. The principle of the interpretation of tongues is to dispense into others what we ourselves have been built up with, that others may also be built up. This is why there should not be any tongue-speaking in the meeting if no one can interpret the tongue. No one should speak anything that builds up himself and not others.

Hence, we must consider others when we meet. It is not how much we say, but whether or not what we say builds up others. Whether or not sisters can ask questions in the meeting is determined by the same principle. Asking questions in the meeting is not just for one's own benefit. It is a matter of whether or not the meeting would be dragged down by such questions. Do you want to help the meeting? The clearest indication of whether or not a man's individuality has been dealt with is seen in the meeting. Some only think of themselves. They have a message in their heart which they want to preach, and they must speak it when they come to the meeting. They have a hymn in their heart which they like to sing, and they will do anything to find an opportunity to sing it. They do not care whether the message will help the meeting or whether the hymn will enliven the congregation. This kind of person brings nothing but damage to the meeting.

Some brothers have been Christians for years, yet they still do not know how to meet. They care little for heaven or earth, the Lord or the Holy Spirit; they only care about themselves. They seem to think that as long as they are present, even alone, they can have a meeting. In their eyes, none of the brothers and sisters exist; they are the only ones who are present. This is truly arrogant. When they speak in the meeting, they want to speak until they are satisfied. In the end they are the only ones who are happy; the other brothers and sisters are all unhappy. They feel that they have a "burden" which must be released. But as soon as they open their mouths, others are forced to pick up this "burden" and take it home with them. Some like long prayers. When they pray, others become tired. When someone breaks the principles of the meeting, the whole church suffers. We must not offend the Holy Spirit in a meeting. Once we offend the Holy Spirit, all the blessing is gone. In the meeting, if we take care of the needs of others and try to build up others, the Holy Spirit will be honored. He will do the building up work, and we will be built up. However, if we do not build up others but talk loosely and offend the Holy Spirit, our meeting will be in vain. When we meet, we should not think of getting something out of the meeting for ourselves. All the activities should be for the benefit of others. If you think your speaking will benefit others, you should speak. If you think your silence will benefit others, remain silent. Always try to take care of others; this is the basic principle of meeting together.

This does not mean that everyone should be silent in the meeting. Many times speaking damages others, but silence also damages others. If you do not care for others, the meeting will suffer whether you speak or remain quiet. Your speaking must be for the benefit of the meeting, and your silence must also be for the benefit of the meeting. Always seek the building up of others. Those who should speak should not remain silent. In the meeting, please remember, "Let all things be done for building up" (1 Cor. 14:26). Everyone should come to the meeting with a goal in mind—he is there for others, not just for himself. We should never do anything that will stumble others. If our silence will stumble others, we should speak. If our speaking will stumble others, we should be silent. We need to learn to speak for the purpose of building up others, and we need to learn to be silent also for the purpose of building up others. Whatever we do, it is for the purpose of building up others, not ourselves. When we are not for ourselves, we will end up being built up ourselves. But when we think only of ourselves, we will not receive any building up.

If you are not sure whether your speaking will build up others, the best thing to do is to check with more experienced brothers. You should ask them, "Do you think I should speak more or less in the meeting?" You have to learn to be a humble person from the beginning. Do not think that you are "somebody." Do not think that you can sing and preach well and that you are great. Please do not make any judgment about yourself. The best thing to do is to ask the experienced brothers. Check with them to see whether your speaking builds up others. Speak more if they encourage you to do so. Speak less if they remind you to speak less. Our meeting will be high if everyone humbles himself to learn from others. When this happens, others will sense that God is in our midst when they come in. This is the result of the operation of the Holy Spirit. I hope we will pay attention to this matter. If we do, our meeting will glorify God.

V. IN CHRIST

Here I should mention another matter. Whenever we meet and whenever we fellowship with one another mutually, we should remember that, as believers, we are one in Christ. Let us read some verses:

First Corinthians 12:13 says, "For also in one Spirit we were all baptized into one body, whether Jews or Greeks, whether slaves or free, and were all given to drink one Spirit." The word *whether* means that there is no distinction. In the Body of Christ there are no worldly distinctions. In one Spirit we were all baptized into one Body and were given to drink one Spirit.

Galatians 3:27-28 says, "For as many as were baptized into Christ have put on Christ. There cannot be Jew nor Greek, there cannot be slave nor free man, there cannot be male and female; for you are all one in Christ Jesus." We were baptized into Christ, and we have also put on Christ. There cannot be Jew or Greek, slave or free man, male or female, because we have all become one in Christ.

Colossians 3:10-11 says, "And have put on the new man, which is being renewed unto full knowledge according to the image of Him who created him, where there cannot be Greek and Jew, circumcision and uncircumcision, barbarian, Scythian, slave, free man, but Christ is all and in all." Both Galatians 3:28 and Colossians 3:11 use the phrase *there cannot be*. There cannot be any distinctions because we have put on the new man; we are being constituted into one new man. This new man is created according to God (Eph. 4:24). In the new man there cannot be Greek or Jew, circumcision or uncircumcision, barbarian or Scythian, slave or free man.

Only Christ is all and in all. There is only one entity, and all have become one.

In reading these three portions of the Scripture, we notice that the believers are one in Christ. In the Lord there is no distinction of past status. In the new man and in the Body of Christ, there is no difference whatsoever. If we introduce these manmade distinctions into the church, the relationship among the brothers and sisters will be shifted to the wrong ground.

We have mentioned five distinctions so far: the distinction between Greek and Jew, between free man and slave, between male and female, between barbarian and Scythian, and between circumcision and uncircumcision.

The distinction between Greek and Jew means two things. First the Jews and the Greeks are two different races; they belong to two different countries. In the Body of Christ, in Christ, and in the new man, there cannot be Jew or Greek. The Jews should not boast that they are descendants of Abraham and God's chosen people, and they should not despise all foreigners. We must realize that both Jews and Greeks have been made one in Christ already. Boundaries no longer exist in Christ. In the Lord all have become brothers. We cannot divide God's children into different classes. In the Body of Christ and in the new man, there is only one entity. If you bring the idea of kinship and regional flavor into the church, you do not know what the church of Christ is. You are in the church now, and you must see that we have no distinction between Jew and Greek here. It is a hard thing for the Jews to give up this distinction. But the Bible says that in Christ there cannot be Jew and Greek. Christ is all and in all. In the church there is only Christ.

There is another distinction between the Jews and the Greeks. Jews have a zealous and religious temperament, while Greeks represent an intellectual temperament. Historically, whenever you speak of religion, people think of the Jews. Whenever you speak of science and philosophy, people think of the Greeks. This is a distinction in character. However, no matter how different their characters are, Jews can be Christians, and Greeks also can be Christians. Those who are zealous for religion can be Christians, and those who are intellectual also can be Christians. In Christ, there is no distinction between Jews and Greeks. One is concerned with the feeling of the conscience, and the other is concerned with reasoning and deduction. Are these two different? According to the flesh, they definitely are different in disposition. One acts according to feelings, and the other acts according to intellect. But in Christ there is no distinction between Jews and Greeks. A warm person can be a Christian, and a cold person also can be a Christian. The one who walks by intuition can be a Christian, and the one who walks by reason also can be a Christian. All kinds of people can be Christians.

Once you become a Christian, you must leave your past temperament behind. There is no such thing in the church. Often the church suffers because many people try to bring their natural flavor and peculiar traits into the church. When those who do not like to talk gather together, they become a quiet group. When those who chatter gather together, they become a chattering group. When those who are cold gather together, they become a group of cold people. When those who are warm gather together, they become a group of warm people. As a result, many distinctions are built up among God's children.

However, there is no place for natural dispositions in the church. In Christ and in the new man, there is no place for natural disposition. Do not think that others are wrong because their disposition is different from yours. You must realize that your own disposition is also unacceptable to others. Whether you are quick or quiet, cold or warm, intellectual or emotional, once you become a brother or a sister, you must put off these things. If you bring these natural elements into the church, they will become the basis of confusion and division. When you bring your disposition and temperament into the church, you will make yourself the standard and the criteria. Those who are up to your standard will be classified as good Christians, and those who are not up to your standard will be classified as poor Christians. Those who get along with your character will be deemed right and those who do not get along with your character will be deemed wrong. When this happens, the church will suffer through your disposition and temperament. Such distinctions must never exist in the church.

The second distinction is between free men and slaves. This distinction has also been eliminated in Christ. In Christ, the distinction between free men and slaves does not exist. Paul wrote the Epistles of 1 Corinthians, Galatians, and Colossians during the Roman era when slavery was practiced. At that time slaves were like animals or tools; they were their masters' possessions. Children born to slaves were automatically slaves; they had no freedom their whole life. The distinction between the free man and the slave was very great. However, God does not allow this distinction to exist in the church. The Epistles of 1 Corinthians, Galatians, and Colossians all say that there cannot be free man or slave. This distinction has been eliminated in Christ.

The third distinction is between male and female. In Christ and in the new man, the male and the female have the same status; there is no distinction between them. The male does not occupy a special position; neither does the female. Because Christ is all and in all, there is no distinction between male and female. In spiritual matters there is no difference between male and female. A brother is saved by the life of Christ, that is, by the life of God's Son. A sister also is saved by the life of Christ, the life of God's Son. The brother has become God's son, and the sister has become God's son as well. In Christ we are all God's sons, and there is no distinction between male and female.

The fourth distinction is between barbarians and Scythians. This is a distinction of culture. There are differences in cultural standards, yet Paul told us that the cultural distinctions of barbarians and Scythians alike have been abolished in Christ.

Of course, we should learn to be a Jew among Jews, and to be as under law to those under law (1 Cor. 9:20-22). Among people of other cultures, we should behave according to their culture. We should learn to be one with all people in all places. When we contact those of a different culture, we should learn to be one with them in Christ. The final distinction is between circumcision and uncircumcision. This distinction has to do with marks of piety in the flesh. The Jews have the mark of circumcision on their bodies. It shows that they belong to God, that they fear God, and that they reject the flesh. Yet they overemphasize circumcision. Acts 15 speaks of some Jews who tried to compel the Gentiles to be circumcised.

Christians also have their "marks of piety in the flesh." For example, baptism, head covering, the breaking of bread, the laying on of hands, and so on can all become marks of piety. Baptism has a spiritual meaning, but it can also be a mark of piety in the flesh. Head covering with the sisters has a spiritual meaning, but it can also be a mark of piety in the flesh. Bread-breaking and the laying on of hands have spiritual meanings, but they can also become marks of piety in the flesh. All of these things have spiritual meaning; they are all spiritual matters. However, we may use these things to separate God's children, boasting about marks which others do not have, and the result is disunity. If we do this, we have downgraded these matters from their spiritual level and made them mere physical marks in the flesh. When this happens, we become, in principle, the same as the Jews who boasted in circumcision; our baptism, head covering, bread-breaking, and hand-laying have become our "circumcision." If we differentiate between God's children based on these things, we have made distinctions according to the flesh. However, in Christ there is no distinction between circumcision and uncircumcision. No physical mark of the flesh can be used to differentiate God's children. In Christ we are made one. The life in Christ is one. All of these things are outside of the life of Christ. Of course, it is good to have the spiritual reality that accompanies these physical marks. But if one has the spiritual reality yet is lacking in the physical marks, we cannot count him out. God's children should not allow physical marks to damage the oneness in the Lord and the oneness in the new man.

We all are brothers and sisters. We are the new man in

Christ. We all are members in the Body, and we all are parts of the Body. Once we are in the church, we should not have any distinction outside of Christ. Everyone stands on new ground. Everyone is in the new man created by the Lord and everyone is in the Body built up by Him. We must see that all of God's children are one. There is no place for superiority or inferiority. We must eliminate the denominational and sectarian thoughts from our hearts. If we do this, there will be no division in the meeting of the church of God and in the fellowship between the saints. We have to pay attention to these matters in the meeting, and we have to live out such a life in our daily walk. May God bless us.